P9-CFS-841

Cinderella

A Random House PICTUREBACK®

for my mother
Katharine Sturges Knight

Copyright © 1978 by Hilary Knight. All rights reserved under International and Pan-American Copyright Conventions. Published in the United States by Random House, Inc., New York, and simultaneously in Canada by Random House of Canada Limited, Toronto.

Library of Congress Cataloging in Publication Data: Cinderella. Hilary Knight's Cinderella. (A Random House pictureback) *Summary:* A mistreated kitchen maid, with the help of her fairy godmother, attends the palace ball on the condition that she leave before midnight. [1. Fairy tales. 2. Folklore—France] I. Knight, Hilary. II. Title. PZ8.C488Kn 1981 398.2'1 [E] 80-18660 ISBN: 0-394-83760-6 (B.C.); 0-394-83759-2 (trade); 0-394-93759-7 (lib. bdg.)

Manufactured in the United States of America 7 8 9 0

Hilary Knight's

Cinderella

Random House New York

Once upon a time, long long ago, there
lived a merchant, his beloved wife,
and their beautiful little daughter.
They were blessed with health, happiness,
and all the good things of life. Their cozy house was
in a lovely valley surrounded by friendly neighbors.
And on a hilltop overlooking the valley stood the palace
of the king and queen and their young son, the prince.

But fate brought a sudden end to the merchant's
blissful life. One day his wife became ill, and
within a week she died.

The merchant and his daughter were grief stricken. But after several years, the merchant began to search for someone with the same qualities as his late wife.

At last he thought he had found her. She was a widow with two young daughters of her own. He married her and brought his new family home with him. His daughter welcomed them happily.

HERE LIES
MY
BELOVED
WIFE

But within a few months, fate struck once more. The merchant was lost at sea on one of his ships. Soon the merchant's daughter discovered the true nature of her new mother and sisters. They were jealous of her beauty and kindness, and forced her to be little more than a servant in her own home. They dressed her in rags and made her sleep in an attic room on a bed of straw.

And they were always ordering her about.

"Fix the tea! Wash the dishes! Sweep the ashes!" they would scold.

Because the poor girl spent her few free hours huddled by the kitchen hearth among the ashes and cinders, they called her Cinderella.

One day, some time later, a messenger from the king brought an invitation to a royal ball. All the eligible young ladies in the land had been asked to attend, for the prince was looking for a bride. Cinderella's wicked sisters immediately began arguing about what they would wear.

Poor Cinderella had nothing but rags. Without a gown, she could not even think of going to the ball.

On the day of the ball Cinderella helped her sisters get dressed.
They did nothing but fuss and fret the whole time.

And when they were ready, they flounced off without even saying good-by.

All alone, Cinderella sat down beside the hearth. "How I wish I could go to the ball," she cried.

Suddenly, into the kitchen flew a most extraordinary person.

"Who are you?" asked Cinderella, drying her eyes.

"I am your fairy godmother, and because you are so kind and good, you *shall* go to the ball tonight!"

"But, Godmother," said Cinderella, "my sisters have taken the carriage, and these rags I'm wearing are my only clothes!"

"No bother!" said the fairy. "We will find everything we need right in the garden. Bring me a pumpkin, one fat rat, two mice, and four lizards!"

Cinderella watched with amazement as her fairy godmother began to chant, giving each of the things she had asked for a tap with her magic wand.

A *plump orange pumpkin*,
I've been told,
Will make a fine carriage
Of crystal and gold!

Little mice, very nice!
They'll be two footmen
In a trice!

Here, old rat, a playful pat!
Now you're a coachman
Jolly and fat!

Lizards will complete our needs,
They'll become four
Stamping steeds!

"Now, Cinderella," ordered the fairy, "fetch me the following:"

Guinea-fowl feathers, and bottles of blue,
Mothwings and cobwebs sprinkled with dew!

I'll mix them with berries and sassafras,
And dress you in gossamer with slippers of glass!

"There!" cried the fairy triumphantly. "You're ready for the royal ball!"

With a cry of joy Cinderella sprang into her carriage.

"Beware, Cinderella!" called her fairy godmother. "You must leave the ball by midnight or the spell will vanish! The carriage and horses, the footmen, your gown—everything will disappear when the clock strikes twelve!"

"I will remember!" called Cinderella, waving good-by.

From the moment Cinderella entered the ballroom, the prince would dance with no other partner. Her wicked sisters did not even recognize her. Everyone wondered who this beautiful stranger could be.

While the orchestra played waltz after waltz, Cinderella danced every one with the prince. She was so happy she did not think about the time. When at last the clock began to strike the hour of midnight, Cinderella scarcely heard it. . . .

Suddenly Cinderella recalled her fairy godmother's warning.
She ran out of the ballroom and flew down the stairs.
The prince tried to follow her, but he found only her tiny
glass slipper, which had fallen from her foot.

At the last stroke of midnight, the spell vanished. Cinderella's gossamer gown disappeared. When she looked for her carriage, there was only a shattered pumpkin shell. All that was left of the fairy's magic was the other glass slipper. Cinderella put it in the pocket of her shabby apron and ran all the way home.

When Cinderella's sisters returned from the ball, they taunted her with stories of the grand time they'd had. They told her about the mysterious stranger, and how the prince had sworn to make her his princess.

"She vanished at midnight," said one sister, "leaving only a tiny glass slipper."

"The prince will search the whole countryside for its owner," said the other, "and she shall be his bride."

The prince himself led the search for the owner of the glass slipper. Although every young lady in the land tried it on, not one could slip her foot into the tiny shoe.

Finally the prince came to Cinderella's house. The first sister tried on the slipper. But it was much too small. The second sister pushed and pulled at the shoe. But try as she might, she could not get the slipper on.

The prince sadly turned to leave. Then he heard a familiar voice coming from the kitchen. "Let me try," said Cinderella. Her stepmother and sisters were horrified when she drew the other slipper from her pocket.

The prince fell to his knees before Cinderella as she easily slipped her foot into the glass shoe. "My princess!" he cried, and he threw his arms around her.

Cinderella married the prince and went to live in the palace. Of course, she forgave her stepmother and sisters and asked them to live with her. From then on, they treated her kindly.

As for Cinderella's fairy godmother, she watched over them constantly... and they all lived happily ever after.